Simple Simon met a pie man
Going to the fair.
Says Simple Simon to the pie man,
"Let me taste your ware."

Says the pie man to Simple Simon,
"Show me first your penny."
Says Simple Simon to the pie man,
"Indeed, I have not any."

Lavender's blue, dilly, dilly,
  Lavender's green.
When I am king, dilly, dilly,
  You shall be queen.
Call up your men, dilly, dilly,
  Set them to work.
Some to the plow, dilly, dilly,
  Some to the cart.
Some to make hay, dilly, dilly,
  Some to cut corn,
While you and I, dilly, dilly,
  Keep ourselves warm.

Old King Cole
Was a merry old soul,
And a merry old soul was he.
He called for his pipe,
And he called for his bowl,
And he called for his fiddlers three.

Polly, put the kettle on,
Polly, put the kettle on,
Polly, put the kettle on,
We'll all have tea.

Pease porridge hot,
Pease porridge cold,
Pease porridge in the pot
Nine days old.
Some like it hot,
Some like it cold,
Some like it in the pot
Nine days old.

Sing a song of sixpence,
    A pocket full of rye,
Four-and-twenty blackbirds
    Baked in a pie.

When the pie was opened,
    The birds began to sing.
Was not that a dainty dish
    To set before the king?

Jack Sprat could eat no fat,
    His wife could eat no lean,
And so between the two of them,
    They licked the platter clean.

Peter Piper picked a peck of pickled peppers.
A peck of pickled peppers Peter Piper picked.
If Peter Piper picked a peck of pickled peppers,
Where's the peck of pickled peppers Peter Piper picked?

There was a little girl, and she had a little curl
  Right in the middle of her forehead.
When she was good she was very, very good,
  But when she was bad she was horrid.

Jack be nimble,
  Jack be quick,
Jack jumped over
  The candlestick.

Here we go round the mulberry bush,
The mulberry bush, the mulberry bush.
Here we go round the mulberry bush,
On a cold and frosty morning.

This is the way we wash our clothes,
Wash our clothes, wash our clothes.
This is the way we wash our clothes,
On a cold and frosty morning.

This is the way we go to school,
Go to school, go to school.
This is the way we go to school,
On a cold and frosty morning.

This is the way we come out of school,
Come out of school, come out of school.
This is the way we come out of school,
On a cold and frosty morning.

Diddle, diddle, dumpling, my son John
Went to bed with his trousers on.
One shoe off, and one shoe on,
Diddle, diddle, dumpling, my son John.

Little Jack Horner
Sat in a corner,
Eating a Christmas pie.
He put in his thumb,
And pulled out a plum,
And said, "What a good boy am I!"

Mary, Mary, quite contrary,
How does your garden grow?
With silver bells and cockleshells,
And pretty maids all in a row.

Little Tommy Tucker
    Sings for his supper.
What shall we give him?
    White bread and butter.
How shall he cut it
    Without e'er a knife?
How can he marry
    Without e'er a wife?

Hush-a-bye, baby, on the tree top,
When the wind blows the cradle will rock.
When the bough breaks the cradle will fall,
Down will come baby, cradle, and all.

Hush, little baby, don't say a word,
Papa's going to buy you a mockingbird.
If the mockingbird won't sing,
Papa's going to buy you a diamond ring.
If the diamond ring turns to brass,
Papa's going to buy you a looking glass.
If the looking glass gets broke,
Papa's going to buy you a billy goat.
If that billy goat runs away,
Papa's going to buy you another today.

Little Miss Muffet
Sat on a tuffet
Eating her curds and whey.
Along came a spider
Who sat down beside her
And frightened Miss Muffet away.

Pat-a-cake, pat-a-cake, baker's man,
Bake me a cake as fast as you can.
Pat it and prick it, and mark it with B,
And put it in the oven for Baby and me.

If all the world was apple pie
And all the sea was ink,
And all the trees were bread and cheese,
What would we have to drink?

I saw a ship sailing,
A-sailing on the sea,
And, oh, but it was laden
With pretty things for thee.

There were cookies in the cabin
And apples in the hold.
The sails were made of silk,
And the masts were all of gold.